The Star Dancer

Jo Brodie

Jo Brodie has asserted her right to be identified as the author of this work in accordance with the Copyright, Designs and Patents Act 1988.

Any resemblance to actual persons, living or dead, is purely coincidental.

DEDICATION

To all the people who rescue animals and love them.
To Brian and Susan who sent the golden key.
For everyone struggling, don't give up.

Buddhism has played a big part in my life, and is reflected in these
stories. Sometimes though, be careful what you wish for....

CONTENTS

ACKNOWLEDGMENTS

The Star Dancer was written after the early death of a friend of mine who was very influential in my life. She was so dedicated to the rescue and welfare of greyhounds and lurchers that it left a profound impression on my life. She was a brave woman and a fearless friend.

I still have the ARK number plate on my mantlepiece, so thank you to whoever sent that to me.

The Star Dancer

The girl on the beach stirred, and stretched slightly, enjoying the lithe feel of her body, and then opened her eyes.

It took her a few moments to establish her surroundings, and she lay still staring up into the sky with it's galaxy of stars burning in the night.

She became aware of the lightness of her body, and the absence of pain, and turned her head to look at the line of her arm and hand lying beside her.

She was fascinated to see that she was now composed of softly glowing shimmering atoms of energy, which flowed within the shape of her body in a gentle mist made up of a myriad of colours.

'How very beautiful' she thought to herself, and lay back to continue enjoying this strange dream.

After a while, a sense of uneasiness settled upon her, and she sat up, drew up her knees and propped her hands under her chin as she took in her surroundings.

She saw mountains in the distance, softly glistening and shape shifting, and became aware that they too were made of light. She sat on a bed of sand, undulating towards a vast stretch of golden beach where a calm sea shushed gently against the sand.

She saw no other person, and as time passed and she sat watching the heavens, a gradual realization came to her that she must have died. Her poor tired cancer riddled body no longer existed except as a pale glimmering haze, and her thoughts were free, with a calmness that had been lacking in the last few days of her life.

She began to think back on her previous life, and got up and made her way slowly along the beach. Memories of her life passed through her mind. She thought of all her goals, her passions in life, her accomplishments, and her mistakes.

She thought of all the unwanted dogs she had saved from certain death, and sadness came into her soul.

'I wish I had done more.'

She thought of all those she had not been able to save. All her life she had tried to help both man and beast, but her passion had been for the unloved dogs, and she had set herself the goal of saving as many as possible, often to the detriment of her finances and relationships.

She sighed as she walked, and the light that was her body flickered and quivered with her thoughts.

She wandered slowly along, thinking about her life and what she had made of it.

'I wish I'd had longer.' She mused, and the waves along the golden shore whispered 'hush, hush' and caressed her ankles.

She walked for some time, time enough to watch a distant shower of meteorites pass by, and as she gazed across the sea she saw a small boat bob slowly towards the shore.

It fetched up against the sand with a bump as it beached itself. Moving closer, she realized it was a small fishing boat, equipped with oars and a sail, which was furled to the mast.

It lay slightly on its side, rolling gently with the movement of the tide, and as she approached she saw the name 'The Star Dancer' painted on its side. Her port of registration was 'The Earth, 699,999,999,251' she noticed with some amusement.

For a while she stood watching it rock softly in the shallows, and then as it seemed to be the right thing to do, she put her hands on the stern and pushed the little boat further into the sea, and climbed on board. Gingerly she sat down, and the sea flowed forward, lifting the boat and taking it back out with the tide.

So settling onto the seat, she set sail from the shores of the earth, towards the oceans of the universe.

Looking over the side of the boat, down into the sea, she realised that the sea was composed of a sea of souls.

Staring down, she saw the ocean lit with bodies of light, flowing around and under The Star Dancer, forming a tide which carried her further away with every wave and dip of the sea. As she watched some lifted an arm as if waving, causing the boat to rock and her to clutch tight to the side.

As the boat dipped and rolled, her clutching hand encountered the end of a fishing rod. She drew it out from where it was stowed and examined it.

It was stowed with what appeared to be a large netted bag made of fine mesh like that of an angler's keep net.

'Never been fishing in my life' she thought and then smiled wryly as she realized that she was not alive in a physical sense any more.

The girl sat for some time, lulled by the movement of the boat, at peace within herself, watching with breathless wonder a star explode in the distant universe, as bright and fiery as a firework display, with fabulous colours swirling in new formations.

Time passed. She had no idea of the days or nights, years or aeons, she was content for it just to be so.

She trailed her hand in the waters of the sea of souls as they propelled The Star Dancer forward, and then sat up with a jerk as she saw a soul float by.

Hastily reaching for the fishing net she scooped the soul out and tipped it into the bottom of the fishing boat.

'Well! What are you doing here?' she exclaimed.

A tail wagged and a long pointy hound nose pushed against her hand. She stroked the lost dog soul, watching its energy shimmer and quiver as she did so.

Happy, the little dog climbed onto the bow of the boat and made itself comfortable.

Suddenly, she understood the purpose of the fishing net.

Avidly she began to search the sea of souls for the lost ones, the ones that she had not been able to save on earth, the ones she could help now.

She scanned the sea and set out to fish for the dog souls, reaching into the sea and scooping out those that she found as they floated by, and over time The Star Dancer began to fill.

Sometimes the sea of souls became tumultuous and she grew to understand that this was due to wars or disasters, natural or otherwise. There would be an influx of souls, and The Star Dancer would bob like a cork, and the sea would become stormy with huge waves.

Occasionally in the distance, she saw other boats on the seas of the universe.

These boats varied hugely, some were merely canoes, the occupant gliding through the water, some were large fishing vessels with crews who threw out the nets daily and then hauled them in every night.

There were boats with single occupants like hers, some fishing with a rod and line, all searching for the souls that they could pull into their boats, according to their passions.

She continued to travel through the universe with her boat full of lost dog souls, all those she had missed on earth, scooped out of the sea of suffering.

Oh and how she loved them! She loved them more with their golden colours and sparkling energy than she had on earth, because they gave her another chance to do more.

As The Star Dancer travelled the oceans flowing past the planets, sometimes the planet would begin to sing softly, and a she would see bright spots of hot energy.

It was the sound and sight of another mortal soul yearning for something to love, crying out for a lost soul to care for.

Then the lost dog souls would become restless, and she would unfurl the sail and set the little boat under way, steering closer. When the Star Dancer sat directly above the planet she would scoop up one of her dogs and gently release them back through the waves, watching as they burnt through the universe to that single bright spot.

She knew when they had arrived as the voice of the planet softened, and a flash of energy sparked like a shooting star.

She was content. The lost dogs would all be loved and cherished, and she knew that they would be reborn in a new body, knowing the love and kindness they had so missed before.

So she travelled, sail unfurled, finding planets which sang softly to her, looking for those who yearned for a new life, and over time her little boat gradually had fewer and fewer occupants.

One day, as The Star Dancer drifted idly, for once empty of lost dogs, a gentle solar wind blew, propelling the little boat forward.

She sat back, watching the swirl of stars from a galaxy, the centre a mass of purple and blue light. Engrossed, she was unaware of the liner which sailed close, until the side gently knocked against the boat, making her grab for the seat.

She suddenly realized that a large hook had been lowered over the side, and she was plucked from the boat, propelled upwards, and hauled in over the side.

'We've got her captain!' came the cry, and a deckhand released her and gave a salute to his captain.

'Welcome aboard!' He smiled at her.

Looking around, she saw it was indeed a liner, full of shimmering souls wandering from deck to deck.

She ran quickly to the side, craning to see The Star Dancer as it bobbed away into the distance. She watched as it drifted further away on the ocean.

'Come over here.' The captain beckoned her closer, walking to the rail and looking down. She followed.

'Look down there. Do you see that?'

Below the gunwale she saw a planet, and then heard its soft cry.

A light burnt fiercer than any laser. The captain turned to her. 'It is a call for you.'

'But I need to do so much more! The dogs need me.' She cried desperately.

The captain shook his head. 'It's your turn now, they are calling for you. Your new life is waiting down there.'

She walked forward, leaning over the rail to see. As she looked into the heart of the light, a force stronger than any magnet began to tug at her, drawing her energy towards it. She looked at the captain.

'Time to go.' He was calm, confident. 'We are all called back when the time is right and now they are calling for you.'

She thought of the little dogs, still floating in the sea, and is if reading her mind the captain spoke again.

'There are others who will be fishing. Nothing is lost, not one will be forgotten.' And he winked at her. He was a kind man.

She nodded slowly, and a deep peace spread through her shimmering body.

She climbed onto the deck rail, looked down into the waving sea of souls, and then with a ripple of light dived off the side, slicing through the waves.

The captain watched as she fell through the stars seeing rays of light being absorbed by the planet below.

To anyone watching it was a magnificent meteor shower in the heavens, as others from the liner joined her.

He smiled and then gave orders for his crew to change direction.

The liner sailed majestically forward towards another small fishing vessel in the distance where the occupant cast a line into the sea.

The planet below sang softly as new life burst forth, to be loved ã
cherished.

The Star Dancer drifted through the seas of the universe, rocking
gently, until the sea of souls dropped it with a little bump against a
perfect golden beach.

A figure of light and energy walked along the sand and stopped
beside the little boat as it lay in the shallows and read the name on the
side.

'The Star Dancer' Port of Registration 'The Earth,699,999,999,252.'

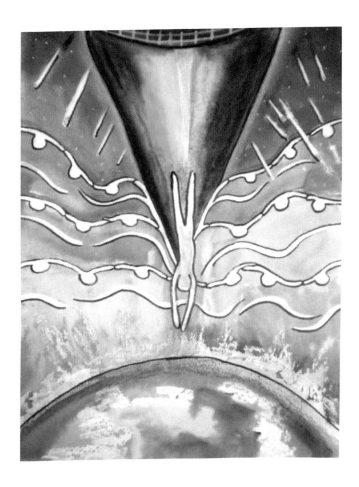

The Snow Queen

, in the heavens, she slumbered, shifting restlessly over the
.s one by one her sisters awoke and drifted down to the earth
,w.

It was not yet her time, but her blood stirred as the seasons changed.

The wind, sensing her awakening, called softly to her.

Beneath her, on the earth, the years passed, and the land became weary and tired.

The wind swirled in recognition that the time had come, and the clouds began to gather, heavy and dark, moving across the sky and obscuring the heavens.

High in the turquoise night sky surrounded by the stars that had been thrown up into the heavens by her mother, the Snow Queen stretched and turned over, her eyes opening.

She was awake.

The wind thrilled at her awakening and picked up speed, blowing across the earth, whispering of her coming.

The clouds dropped closer to the earth, calling to the trees, the animals, and the birds. Some of people who could still hear the sounds of the earth paused, listening, wondering what was being foretold.

The clouds groaned with the weight of the snow, coming together as if in support, ready for the new birth of snowfall.

And all the time the wind moved over the land, whispering, whispering, sometimes it's voice rising to a howl to awaken the slumbering.

'She is awake! She is awake!' it called, and then moved on.

The wind made its way into the forest, stirring the dried beech le: that lay in a carpet beneath the trees, circling in little eddies so that the leaves floated into the air, danced briefly, then sank back to the forest floor.

Hidden deep beneath the ground the unicorns roused, ears flickering. The wind moved in a caress above them.

'She is coming! She is coming!' and the very air thrilled to this knowledge.

The unicorns moved their heads, stretching their necks.

'Soon…Soon…' the wind said, and moved on, coiling through the trees and reviving all the snow creatures that awaited the coming of their Queen.

In the dark night sky the Snow Queen gathered her mantle to her and looked down to the earth. The clouds laden with snow were beneath her and she looked at the clear stars and moon above them.

It was time.

Raising her arms she stepped forward and began to drop slowly down through the heavens, her skirts made from the stars and snowflakes billowing around her.

As she fell gently through the night sky, the temperature began to fall. The clouds gave a sigh of relief, and in the darkness of the night, at last, the snow began to fall.

The snow fell swiftly, silently, steadily as if with a purpose, and began to cover the earth with whiteness.

Gradually as the land became covered all sounds were silenced.

The birds ceased their calls and stilled on their perches. Stock animals gathered together, their breath like a mist in the dark.

was coming and they waited for her arrival with wind to accompany the snowfall.

.oods, the snow covered the autumn leaves, the tracks, .rees. The branches laden with snow formed archways, ..ng new pathways never seen before.

The unicorns felt the arrival of the deep snow, and snorting with effort, began to emerge from the earth, arching their necks and shaking their manes and tails free.

With a surging lunge they were on their feet, and stepping through the forest on silent hooves.

Nearby, white rabbits emerged from their burrows, blinking in the bright snowfall, for theirs had been a long sleep.

A pair of white doves gave a call to each other and swooped through the trees after the unicorns.

And then there she was!

Stepping through the forest the unicorns went to her side, and they walked soundlessly through the bower of snow laden trees that arched above her, forming a canopy for her passing.

The Snow Queen smiled as she saw the snow creatures emerging, and looked around at her white kingdom with wondering eyes.

 An enchanted forest unfolded before her as she walked, passing through the trees and down to the valleys below.

As she moved forward the snow fell faster, thicker, blanketing the mountains, the hills, the towns, the roads, sweeping along in her wake.

She strode through her kingdom, starting in the North where the wind blew the snow into blizzards and sent drifts across the land, and then moving steadily South.

She watched as the Sun tried to rise and break through the clouds as morning dawned, but her magic and power was too great for him, for still the snow fell.

The clouds greedily hugged the earth, spilling their snow, eager to see the Snow Queen as she passed through the land.

She paused briefly to watch the children emerge from their cosy houses, shrieking with delight, and she sat on the hills beside them as they pulled sledges from sheds and used them to slide down the slippery slopes of her snow laden hills.

 As she walked through the land, the white animals came to greet her, bowing on one knee in reverence, staring at the unicorns at her side with their glittering manes made of snow and ice. There had been many stories telling of these beautiful creatures, but no living animal had ever seen them.

She climbed to the tops of mountains, and stood high in the clouds as the snowstorms blew around her, surveying her kingdom below.

The Snow Queen watched as people tried to go about their daily business, ignoring her beautiful snow bound magical land.

She sighed as the cars came to grief, sliding into each other, observing the snow ploughs head out over her hills.

With a wave of her hand she sent snow drifts across the major roads, making the plough's efforts ineffectual.

And slowly the roads began to close, and the railways began to be silenced. As she moved further South, for the first time that anyone could remember, London creaked and groaned, and became still, eerily quiet as buses stopped, trains stopped, cars stopped. The planes taxied to a halt on the snow covered runways.

Such is the rarity of the Snow Queen and her magic power that she had almost been forgotten, and now the people gasped in wonder and amazement as the Capital city ground to a halt, and she passed silently through.

She stared at the frozen lakes surrounded by a glittering cloak of ice and snow, amazed at their beauty. She loved the reflections of the city lights, the snowmen who doffed their hats as she walked by, and the abundance of life fascinated her.

She made her way to the coast and stood on the high white cliffs of Dover looking across the grey and heaving ocean, seeing the clouds greet the sea below with a frozen kiss. How beautiful indeed is her land.

Always by her side paced the unicorns, the white rabbits lopped along, swans flew in her wake, and the white animals gathered.

She walked the length and breadth of her land, and still the snow fell, schools remained closed, shops shut, and the roads were silent, all sounds muffled.

Then one morning the wind joined her.

'He will rise soon.' It whispered in her ear, and her heart gave a little kick, for she stood in the mountains, restless, waiting for the Sun to gather his power and join her.

She saw the clouds begin to drift away little by little, and the morning sky lightened to a powder blue, and then the Sun rose.

He called to her, and flung his arms wide spreading orange and yellow through the sky. He threw a carpet of glittering ice diamonds across the snow for her to walk on, and made icicles of breath taking beauty for her to adorn herself with.

He rose high in the sky, dazzled by her, making her kingdom shimmer with golden brilliance over the frozen snow.

His heart lifted and burnt brightly, bringing warmth to the land. She had waited for him, and he answered her patience by spreading sunshine far and wide.

She understood his offer to bring spring to the earth again, to renew its beauty, and all day he cast warmth and light around her.

The unicorns stayed in the trees, still heavy with snowfall, standing quietly. The Snow Queen watched the Sun's courtship, and waited for the day to pass.

As the Sun sank back down towards the ground he lit the sky with streamers of reds, pinks and yellows. She stepped forward to greet him in the dusk of the day, with the last of the snow clouds drifting about her.

The wind stirred in the trees and snow began to fall from the branches. In the very darkest time of the night, with the chill of the frost all around, the Snow Queen returned.

The unicorns stepped close to her side. She began to make her way steadily back through her kingdom, sometimes stopping to admire the twinkling lights from the silent towns, or to touch the snow covered houses with a caring hand.

She reached the forest where she had first drifted down from the heavens and where the snow was already beginning to retreat. The Snow Queen turned to the unicorns.

They bowed low on one knee to her, and then with a sigh they lay down closing their eyes. Within seconds they were still silent shapes beneath the snow that she cast upon them, mounds in the earth, hidden deep in the frozen ground once again.

The white rabbits hopped away, scratching out their burrows and lying down to sleep until the next Snow Queen arrived.

The doves settled back onto their perches, becoming invisible in the dark.

The Snow Queen climbed to the hills and stood looking across her frozen earth for miles. She stared up to the heavens where the sky was a midnight blue, filled with glittering stars.

She waited for a long time, just watching, for her time in her kingdom was nearly at an end.

And at last, just before the Sun rose to refresh the earth, she threw a handful of snow flakes and stars high into the sky, saw them settle and form bright constellations with clusters of coloured stars.

She smiled at their beauty, and then turned and made her way back into the forest.

With the Sun's power beginning to lighten the sky, the Snow Queen slowly faded into the camouflage of the snowy forest.

The Sun rose and sent the wind to call for his beautiful Snow Queen, searching across the land, melting the snow and bringing warmth back to the frozen land.

The Sun could not find her and so he climbed high in the sky and as he looked down from the high heavens, he saw snowdrops springing up from the earth in every footstep that she had taken.

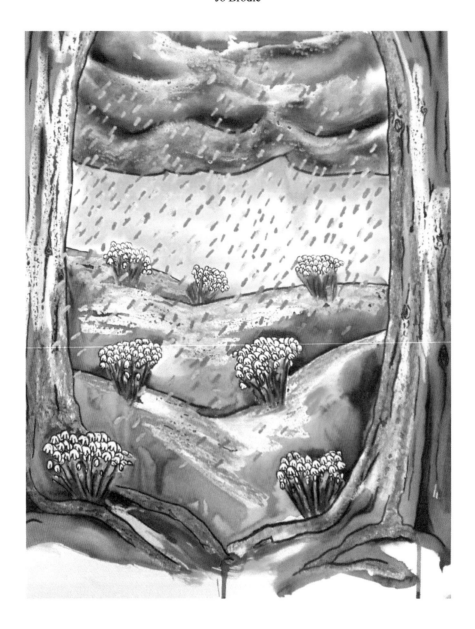

He understood at last that she had gone, that her reign of the Earth was over, and the clouds gathered and cried the Sun's tears down upon the earth.

But as the seasons changed through the years, passing through spring and summer, the redness of autumn and the bitter cold of winter, high in the heavens where she had thrown them, the Snow Queen's daughters slumbered and then stirred, waiting for the time when the earth called to them once more.

The Heaven Diaries

Time passes differently in heaven.

When the greyhound first arrived it took him a little time to get his bearings, and of course there were new companions to get to know, and to play with.

He discovered that in heaven there was no shortage of anything he needed.

The breeze caressed him lightly, and the warmth of the sun was kind on his spirit.

Without his old weary body left behind on the earth, his youthful spirit soared like a skylark, and he became young again.

He greeted old playmates who had gone into the heavens before him, and together they roamed through heaven until they found a good vantage point where they could look down on the earth below.

The greyhound and his companions watched their owner as she continued her life on earth.

Each day that passed without her the greyhound recorded in his heart, like the pages in a diary, for he loved and missed her.

When the night fell on the earth the dogs rose from where they sat watching, and they would wander through the dreamy landscape, chasing rabbits and splashing through ponds.

Sometimes they would see the clouds thicken, and a still timeless quality would hang in the air. The noises in the heavens would quieten, and sounds became muted.

Dogs would gather and wait, exuberance curbed, peering into the mist until one of them rushed forward with a joyous bark to disappear into the dense clouds.

The greyhound waited for them to return after they had vanished into the fog, but they never came back.

He was told that the owners of these dogs had come for them, and that together they had gone further into heaven.

So as the time passed, quickly on earth and slowly in heaven, the greyhound listened to his companion's stories, and then told his own.

He told them of his life as a new born; the snugly warmth of his mother's side and the soft sounds of her breathing. He remembered the feel of her tongue as she washed their blind faces, and the scrape of the straw that they lay on.

The greyhound had been well fed and looked after, and he grew quickly and was soon found a home.

He was taught to hunt and spent several years with one man where he worked hard for his keep, but as injury and age crept upon him, he became slower, and passed from man to man.

Each time his life became poorer, his conditions a little worse. The hands that hit became harder, and the boots that kicked became more painful.

He told his companions of his loneliness, of the cold kennels and the harshness of his owners, until one day he was sold once again, and his misery was complete.

His new owner used him for hunting, but when it became clear that the greyhound was no longer fast or agile enough, although he tried so hard, he was shut in the back yard and left behind.

The rains came and soaked him to the very bone and the cold wind chilled him until he was numb, for there was not even a kennel for him to take shelter in.

When he cried out his despair the man came from the house and kicked him hard enough to wind him and leave him cowering on the concrete floor.

Days passed, and the greyhound began to starve, for no one fed him, or looked kindly upon him.

The greyhound's tale continued, and he spoke of the weeks that passed, surviving on water from the rain, and the odd scrap that was flung from the house.

When he was too weak to move about, he curled into a ball and waited with dull eyed misery for his spirit to leave his body.

And on that day, the gods of the heavens looked down and saw him, and frowned, for it was not yet his time to come to heaven.

The wind was sent to blow mightily upon the land, and opened the yard gate with a gust that stirred the greyhound, and sent him staggering to his feet to take his first steps to freedom.

For a week he roamed free, surviving by scavenging through dustbins, this once proud and joyous hound brought low by starvation and cold.

He tried to avoid people for he had learnt that they brought pain and fear, but it was to no avail, as one day the dog warden came with his noose and chased and caught him.

He was taken to the council pound, and there he discovered that he had seven days to be rehomed, or his life would be at an end.

The greyhound did not care anymore. His spirit was tired and beaten and his body was frail and sore.

He lay in the kennels and waited for the final day.

No one looked at him, although all around dogs came and went.

On the seventh day he sat at the back of the kennels as the last few visitors passed through.

A woman came to the door and clicked her fingers.

He did not stir, or lift his head, for his misery was nearly at an end, and he waited for the vet to come and release him.

She called to him again, and at last he looked at her.

For a moment they stared at each other and something passed between them, before his head dropped to his bed again.

He heard her breath go in on a sharp gasp and her hand clutched to her heart. She said suddenly, 'Oh good heavens! Oh how awful, you poor, poor lad!'

The gods in the heavens above heard her cry out, and sent a swift wind to rattle the cage door and swirl around her ankles as she stood staring in, trying to coax the greyhound to his feet. The wind chilled the greyhound and he came to his feet, shaking.

Within minutes, or so it seemed to the greyhound, the woman left and returned with a lead and collar, and he was being led out from the kennels as fast as his rickety frame could take him.

He was bundled into the back of a car, and as he lay trembling in fear on the back seat, she laid a hand gently on his gaunt spine and said, 'I give you my vow you will never suffer again in your life.'

She got into the car and drove away with him.

The greyhound's heart sank low for he had thought his sufferings were over, and he had no courage left to face his next ordeal.

His new owner took him to her home.

When he was lifted from the car and led inside he screamed with terror, as he had never been allowed in a house before, and he shook and trembled.

Other dogs surrounded him, sniffing him, barking, and nearby a cat hissed with outrage.

He was led into a warm front room and shown a bed which he collapsed into.

The woman bustled about and came to him with a bowl of soft food which she hand fed to him. Confused and exhausted, he was glad when a soft blanket was thrown over him, and he was left to burrow his head deep into the first warm bed he had known since puppyhood.

He closed his eyes and shut everything out.

The greyhound paused in his tale, and his companions huddled closer, comforting him.

He looked into the night sky, and then down to the earth where his owner lay sleeping. The dogs lay down together as they kept their vigil and he continued with his story.

That day marked the beginning of a change so great in his life that the heavenly gods smiled as they watched over him.

It took many months, and many visits to the vet, but he began to fill out and put weight back on as his food was regular, tasty and constant for his needs. His coat became sleek again, his scars healed, and his terror receded.

For the remainder of his life on the earth he was never cold, and he was never hungry. He was never beaten, or hurt. He was never in despair or scared and lonely.

He began to enjoy the walks through the woods, and ran along sandy beaches and played in the sea.

He lay in the sun in the summer months, and curled into his bed with a blanket to cover him in the cold of the winter.

He knew how to lay boneless before a log fire, and he mastered the art of sneaking onto his owner's bed at night without even waking her.

The greyhound learnt about treats, holidays, and kindness. He learnt what enjoyment was, he learnt about love, and he learnt about trust.

His owner had hands that were kind and soothed him, and boots that were only for walking. She stroked and fussed over him, and gradually he understood that life was good to him now, and that he never need be afraid again.

In the first year of their time together he avoided her touch as much as possible. In the second year he discovered that his tail could wag, and wiggle his whole body when she came close to him. In the third year he enjoyed every minute with her, never leaving her side, closer than her own shadow.

He looked forward to their walks, the quiet evenings, the feel of her hands absently stroking his smooth coat, and the sound of her voice.

He had many long contented years with his owner, and he grew old and grey, then older and more tired. Their walks together became shorter, and he spent long hours asleep on the settee or dozing with his head on her knee.

Then one day, the heavens began to call softly to him, and he knew his time on earth was nearly over.

As she had done from the first day that she had seen him, his owner remained at his side until the heavenly gods came for him, and he left his body on earth and soared to the heavens.

He rose to his feet as his story ended, for the sun was rising on the earth and a strawberry sky was spreading across the land.

He stood to watch over his owner as she awoke, as she had once watched over him.

The days in heaven continued, and the years passed on earth. The greyhound played and ran through the hills, and waited patiently.

Then one day the clouds began to thicken, and the silence of the mist descended.

The dogs gathered, and the greyhound strained to see through the thick fog and his ears pricked as he listened.

Softly, through the swirling brightly lit clouds he saw a figure walking steadily and surely towards him, and his gaze became intent.

He glanced at his old playmates who had gathered beside him, and then suddenly with a joyous bark he sprang forward, tail wagging and wagging.

The woman knelt with a laugh and flung open her arms to him as he raced forward through the fog towards her.

He felt her arms close tight round him. Behind him, he heard his companions bark with excitement and run after him as they realised it was their owner who had come for them.

He had waited so patiently for her, as she had once waited for him, for not once in life had he left her side.

Together, with the dogs playing around her feet and the greyhound pacing proudly at her side, they began to walk further into the mist, towards a deeper part of heaven.

Rupert Roobarb and the Ark

There was a woman once who lived in a little flat in a small town, who was very discontented with her life, and so waking up one morning she decided, as in all the old fairy tales, to set out to seek her fortune.

And as in all these fairy tales what she actually achieved was something very different…

She lived in the South, and had spent many years working hard and paying her bills, and had begun to be very bored with being poor.

She was a Buddhist, and she prayed every day for something to change in her life so she could have her own home and have money.

She was also lonely after her little dog died, and so after some time had passed, the gods in the heavens noticed and looked down upon her life.

One of the gods pulled his chair closer to his desk and looked towards the queue of souls waiting at checkpoint 'D.'

'Next!' He called, and a soul approached the desk.

The god shuffled through his papers and his glasses settled on his nose. 'OK, we have a vacancy on Earth with this woman.'

The soul looked down at the planet Earth and said, 'I'm not going back as a dog!'

The god cleared his throat and looked over his glasses with steely eyes at the soul. 'Well, there is nothing else at the moment. If you would like to go to the back of the queue…?'

The soul scowled back at the queue which stretched into infinity and turned back to the god.

'Oh, all right, if I must.' Was the grumpy reply. 'I don't want a silly name though.'

The god smiled and allowed the soul to pass by and disappear with a flash of energy on to Earth.

There was a mumble of voices in the queue, and the god turned back.

'Now calm down everyone please. I know these are difficult times, but you will all get something in time, you just have to be patient.'

He looked through the universe, checking through the planets for a vacancy, and then shuffled his papers.

'Next!'

Below, on Earth, the woman looked at a lurcher puppy sitting on her feet in the rescue centre, and said. 'Well, that seems to have settled it. You had better come home with me, Mr Fred.'

After that the whole of the South seemed to become a very small place for a woman with a large lurcher puppy intent upon causing havoc.

There were various incidents with Mr Fred as he was a very naughty, accident prone puppy enjoying his new life.

These including running through the open front door of a complete stranger's house covered in mud from the local pond, onto their beautiful, newly laid, white carpets.

He also tried to eat a bee and had to be rushed to the vets as his mouth and tongue swelled instantly. A little brush with a dog on the beach left him with twenty three stitches in a shoulder wound, and so it went on.

These finally culminated one sunny morning with one very angry red faced man shouting abuse, two giggling children, and a kite rapidly disappearing into the distance at top speed across the ground with a very happy lurcher puppy holding the tail of it between his teeth.

The woman began to feel rather frazzled by these incidents.

As she had family and friends living in the North, where there was a lot of space for a lively puppy, she felt encouraged to think about a move there.

Many days later after poring over the newspapers and unable to afford any place to rent or buy in the South, she packed her bags, loaded the car, stuck Mr Fred in the back with all the house plants and set on her way to the North.

She had decided to try to make her fortune in an area where she could afford to buy a house, and set herself a target of ten years before returning to the South. She imagined coming home after those ten years with the house sold and money in her pocket for a deposit on a property, and wearing a big smile.

When she arrived and walked into the little house she had rented on a temporary basis, she unpacked, unloaded Mr Fred, and got ready for her new life.

She awoke the next morning to a fog so thick she could not see the hundred yards down the road to the end of the street. Everything was shrouded and dripping. Her heart sank a little, but she was a determined sort of person and not afraid of a few set backs, and so she got on with her life.

She found a job, and began to settle into her new environment.

After a few weeks she had a surprise visit from her family who were now moving back to the South - a new job had beckoned.

After a couple of months she had another surprise visit from her friend who had decided to get married and live happily ever after.

She felt very alone. The woman blew her nose, wiped her tears and took Mr Fred out for a walk.

Several months later she knew she had made a BIG mistake. But being a positive person with a strong faith and a belief in karma, she felt she must have made the causes to be there and so gritted her teeth and made the best of it.

She bought a little house right out in the country and threw herself wholeheartedly into repairing it. It would be an adventure she decided.

Every time she became low in spirits, the god looked down from his desk in the heavens, spotted a vacancy, and then shuffled his papers.

And so it was that the dogs arrived one by one.

First there was Potty Lottie who was mad as a box of frogs, then the Pied Piper, the sweetest soul. Then Bonita Moskita an absolute saluki madam, who arrived to keep all the others, and Mr Fred, who adored her, occupied and busy with little time to worry about anything very much.

The little house was full of mischief and needed constant repairs. In the summer the wind blew ceaselessly, rattling the windows and finding every way of bringing in a draught.

She mended, replaced and fixed constantly. The house played pranks and undid every repair, even finding new problems for the woman to sort out.

A favourite trick was to slide slates off the roof in the dead of night so that she nearly jumped out of her skin.

In the winter the snows came, along with the freezing cold, and the wind blew ceaselessly, whistling and howling round the house.

A few years drifted by.

She walked the dogs across fells and around reservoirs, through forests and ancient castle remains. She determinedly admired the severe beauty of it all, the harshness and toughness of the life and environment, and she prayed that her Buddhist faith would help her overcome all her difficulties.

Watching her from the heavens the god shuffled his papers together and tapped them on the desk as a soul in the front of the queue became very persistent.

'Me! Me! Me next!' it cried, jumping up and down to be noticed.

'Next!' came the call, and the soul stepped eagerly forward.

'We don't really have a vacancy,' said the god. 'However, it may be possible to fit you in there with Mr Fred who is looking for an apprentice to train up, but it could be that there just isn't enough space. I suggest you take it, and we shall see how you get on.'

So one sharp winter's morning, on the Earth, the woman received a phone call about a young lurcher in desperate need of help.

Off she went to collect another rescue dog, and Rupert Roobarb joined the others in his new family.

It would be fair to say that his arrival in the group was not entirely successful. He was young and wild and full of nonsense, had no idea about anything, and the nick name of 'that little twit' was used quite often. He knew how to run very fast in the opposite direction of the one required and not much else. Although very sweet natured he barely had a brain cell to rub together.

The woman was busy working and sorting out the dogs and the cats. The cats had also arrived via the gods - perhaps to cause as much mayhem as possible as the gods liked a good belly laugh.

There was Psycho Cat Izzie who never accepted that he had returned in a cat's body and as a kitten hung from Mr Fred's face by his claws. He spat and hissed before attacking everyone.

Then along came the lovely Fenella, who quickly realized how lucky she was as she got another nine lives.

The woman thought endlessly about going home but could not imagine how to do it with all the animals. No, she decided, grit your teeth and get on with it then take the money and run.

Then one morning as she was listening to the radio, she heard the term 'credit crunch' for the first time in relation to the American economy.

She stroked Mr Fred's ears as she listened. Rupert Roobarb came over and looked at her with anxious brown eyes.

'It won't affect us' she told him confidently 'I should be all right as I can manage the mortgage.'

The gods looked down in some surprise at this confident statement. And because all the gods in the heavens have different personalities, when the god at check point 'D' took his break, another stepped in, and thought, ' I wonder what will happen if I do this?...'

So scarcely had the words left her mouth than the credit crunch began to hit Britain.

At first she was not worried. She could pay the mortgage on the house. But after a while the bills began to be higher, prices for everything went up and she began to struggle.

She got a second job, then a third, and ran about like a headless chicken in between.

Then the winters took a turn for the worse. Prices for fuel rocketed as the temperatures plummeted and the wind blew unkindly in endless gales, bitter and with violent force.

The woman battened down the hatches and sat tight through the long winters. The snows fell, the wind blew for months and months, and along came the coldest winter she had ever lived through.

The dogs wore knitted jumpers in the house, and were covered up with blankets in their beds. It was so cold she leapt into her bed with all her clothes on, and the dogs decided to join her under the duvet. No one wanted to get out from underneath it so sleep was a mesh of human and dogs together.

She and the dogs wrapped up in layer after layer when they went out, staggering through feet of snow.

Her hair froze as she walked, and the dogs cut themselves falling through the ice.

They unwrapped when they went in and wrapped up again quickly in woolly jumpers, thick fleeces and blankets, and she became the proud possessor of a pair of long johns.

She dug the car out every morning and went off to work and began the same thing again the next day.

These were long, long winters. When the spring finally arrived the woman was exhausted and felt as if she had begun to go slightly mad. For a while sanity returned as the weather improved.

She walked the dogs and admired the scenery once again with a grim resolve that she would enjoy it.

The wind blew night and day, through every summer with a churlish disinclination to become a light breeze. In the winter it revved up to storm force, thrilled by its own power.

Scarcely had the summer arrived than it would be winter just round the corner.

The woman became more and more unhappy. She took to railing at the gods when she was walking, especially at the wind, which blew harder with every curse she flung at it.

The calendar clicked through another year, and nine years gradually crept through until her goal of ten years arrived.

One day as she sat praying doing her morning Buddhist recital, she had a light bulb moment and finally admitted to herself:

'I absolutely hate it. I HATE IT!' and she got up and sang and played with the dogs, singing at the top of her voice 'I hate it I hate it!' because it was a relief to finally say it out loud.

'I will sell the house and go home' she thought to herself 'I have been here ten years!' and promptly rang the local estate agents and put the house up for sale.

Alas, little did she realize quite what the credit crunch meant in terms of selling a property. She became sunk in gloom as no buyer came forward, and time rolled on.

Then that summer, the rains came. Day in, day out, night after night, day after day. It rained. And it rained. It was biblical the way it rained.

The house became a laundry of wet dog coats, wet towels, dripping waterproofs, and wellingtons. The cats stared out from rain splattered windows onto soaked and sodden land.

Everyday the woman got up and walked the dogs through the rain and the wind on the fells.

One day as she was walking, with the four older dogs trailing sullenly behind her, she raised her fists to heavens and yelled,

'Oh ye gods, stop the rain. If you can do anything at all stop it bloody raining!'

She paused for a moment, but the heavens opened up and rained harder.

Totally dispirited she picked up a stick and threw it for Rupert Roobarb the only one who was desperately trying to enjoy himself at the front of the pack.

It was at this point that the god returned from his break and looked down to see what was going on.

He turned to the other god who was trying to look innocent and as if he had not been interfering, and frowned at him. 'What have you been doing?'

'I just wanted to see what would happen if I did that.'

The god turned back, and wrote something on a white slip of paper and dropped it over the edge of the desk.

It floated down through the heavens. He smiled, not very nicely, at the other god. 'Now we shall see what happens next.' He said.

On Earth, Rupert Roobarb darted off, still determined to enjoy his very wet walk. Of course he couldn't find the stick, but he picked up something white and similar in shape and bounced back to the woman with it, happy to please her.

'What have you got there Rupert Roo?' she asked him, wiping the water from her face.

He dropped it and stood back.

The woman bent down and turned it over. For a moment she was totally still.

'It's a sign.' She whispered and stared again at the thing she held in her hand. It was part of a number plate; the heavens only knew how it came to be there.

On it was written:

ARK

She leant forward and gave Roo a big kiss and began to laugh.

'It's a sign!' She shouted, her face raised to the pouring rain, and then she ran up and down the track dancing and waving her fists in the air splashing through the puddles while the older dogs looked on with some surprise. 'It's a sign! Thank you, gods!'

She tucked the sign into her pocket and headed back up the long hill on the fell, trudging along with her head full of thoughts.

An Ark.

Did that mean it would never stop raining? Did she have to build one? How do you build an Ark? She was uneasily aware that she was not a carpenter, and not very good at DIY. There must be a way she determined.

And so it began.

Every night after work, the woman returned, sorted out all the animals and thought about how to build an Ark.

Because she had no idea, each day she sat and did her Buddhist practice and asked the universe for inspiration on how to make an Ark.

In it she could take all her animals and sail away back to the South, back to her home.

She hardly slept in her anxiety, her mind in turmoil. She began to look at houses in the South in the areas where she could perhaps settle.

Daily she prayed to the universe to help her find something.

'There must be a house somewhere in the South where the landlord will not mind my animals. There must be one house out there somewhere!' and she chanted and prayed and thought about the Ark.

The woman decided that the little house of mischief she was living in had to be sold no matter what, and took steps to do that. The house was not very amused as it liked playing its pranks, but the woman took this in her stride.

She realized that she wasn't going to make her fortune as she had thought all those years ago - that damn credit crunch! – but found she could not find it in her heart to care very much about it.

The most important thing for her was to return home with her animals who were all getting older, if no wiser.

'We all go, or we all stay' she told them as they sat close to the fire watching her working on designs for the Ark, 'and as we are not staying, we are all going.'

She was determined and remembered some less than favorable comments about her character. 'Pig headed' her mother used to say. 'Stubborn as a mule' another friend remarked. Not always good qualities, but very useful at times, and this appeared to be one of them.

One morning she took a very deep breath and handed her notice in at work.

She was quite scared because she still had not made the Ark, but she knew it was time to go.

'Now or never!' she cried to the dogs as she marched across the fell.

She went back to the house and all evening her neighbours listened and wondered at the sounds of hammering and sawing wood coming from inside.

The god watched for a while, pleased with her progress. He could see that some of the souls he had sent down to her were now in older bodies, struggling with the weather and sore bones, and he understood her determination to return home to a warmer environment and a kinder life for them.

Perhaps she deserved a little helping hand, he mused to himself.

So, one morning, the post arrived and in it was a small packet with her name on it. She opened it and stood in silence, just staring.

A golden key lay in her hand with a small tag attached, with the number of a house written upon it.

Her fingers closed tightly round it, and she breathed the word 'Freedom.'

It was really a little yellow Yale key to a terraced property but to her it was golden and the key to her new life.

She placed the key on her Buddhist altar with barely suppressed relief and thanked the universe for providing her with her new home.

She continued to build the Ark with renewed energy. Day and night she worked with the sound of drills and hammering filling the air along with muffled shrieks and curses as she hit her thumbs by mistake.

One night after walking the dogs, there was an air of excitement about her.

All day the furniture had disappeared leaving the house empty and grumpy. She cleaned it from top to bottom, making sure the house was spotless, which improved its mood somewhat.

Then in the dead of night, she loaded the dogs and the cats into the Ark she had built. She rolled it quietly out into the street, checked the sails and lashed the tarpaulin down.

She posted the keys to the house back through the letter box, and as the heavens opened, she steered the boat away, on the swell of the water, leaving the house, the fell, and all thoughts of making her fortune behind her.

She sailed the Ark all night, through the rain and the darkness until the dawn broke and the light spread through the sky.

Rupert Roobarb sat beside her, the older dogs slept under the tarpaulin, and in her hand she clutched the golden key.

It was a long voyage through the storm, but as the sun rose high and the rain ceased, she could see she had nearly reached the end of her journey.

The little boat came to rest against the kerb in a new city, beside a small yellow house with the early morning sun warming it. She heard the cry of seagulls above, and knew she had finally made it home.

She climbed down from the Ark and secured the mooring ropes. With a shaky breath she stepped forward and fitted the golden key into the lock on the door and listened to the click as it unlocked. The door swung open and she took a deep breath and stepped through.

The animals wriggled out from beneath the tarpaulin, and two by two followed her through the open front door and into their new lives.

So you see in the end, it wasn't all about money. She had set sail on an adventure; to seek her fortune, but what she didn't realize was that riches come in many forms.

The woman's good fortune in the end was being able to be close to all the things she loved and that included her animals.

No fairy story would be complete without its happy ending.

The god in the heavens smiled, rather pleased with the results. He looked at his watch and thought it was time for his lunch break. The queue of souls muttered darkly and fidgeted before settling down again.

Tidying his desk he put the papers for the afternoon in the drawer and strolled away.

Another god, at another desk and another checkpoint, looked down through the universe at another planet, and thought, 'I wonder what will happen if I do this…?'

ABOUT THE AUTHOR

Jo Brodie lives and works in West Sussex.

She is an artist and writes and illustrates her own short stories which can be found on Amazon and Kindle ebooks.

She supports Greyhound and Lurcher rescue groups, the PDSA, and charities that she has a personal interest in.

Her life changed dramatically upon the introduction of a lurcher puppy called Mr Fred, in ways that she could not believe!

She has been a Buddhist for over 35 years.

Her paintings can be found on her Etsy shop: jobrodieart

Available as a paperback:

The Dog Tails
Hounded!
The Singing Gates

ebooks:

The Dog Tails
Hounded
The Singing Gates

Printed in Great Britain
by Amazon